The SOMETIMES GIANT

by Sam Lewis-Williams

Andersen Press

London

for Kim, Vashti and Tess

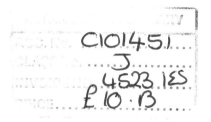

Copyright © 1998 by Sam Lewis-Williams
The rights of Sam Lewis-Williams to be identified as the author and illustrator of this work
have been asserted by him in accordance with the Copyright, Designs and Patents Act, 1988.
First published in Great Britain in 1998 by Andersen Press Ltd., 20 Vauxhall Bridge Road, London SW1V 2SA.
Published in Australia by Random House Australia Pty., 20 Alfred Street, Milsons Point, Sydney, NSW 2061.
All rights reserved. Colour separated by Fotoriproduzioni Grafiche, Verona.
Printed and bound in Italy by Grafiche AZ, Verona.

10   9   8   7   6   5   4   3   2   1

British Library Cataloguing in Publication Data available.

ISBN 0 86264 832 7

This book has been printed on acid-free paper

Harry loved climbing trees.
One day, he found a tree taller than
any he had ever seen. He started climbing,
higher and higher, up and up, until . . .

. . . he reached the top and found himself
inside a castle. A little man was sitting
at a table, drinking a cup of tea.
  "What's the idea, climbing up my
beanstalk uninvited?" said the little man.

"Beanstalk?" said Harry. "I thought it was a funny tree!"
"There's nothing funny about my beanstalk, young Jack,"
said the little man. "Follow me!"

"I don't mean to be rude," said Harry politely,
"but if that is a beanstalk, shouldn't you be a giant?"
"That's it," said the little man. "I'm the giant,
you're Jack and your mum's got a cow."

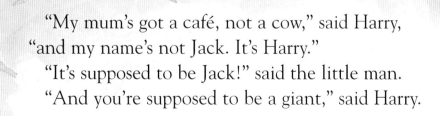

"My mum's got a café, not a cow," said Harry,
"and my name's not Jack. It's Harry."
"It's supposed to be Jack!" said the little man.
"And you're supposed to be a giant," said Harry.

"I am a giant," said the little man. "Sometimes."
"How can you be a giant sometimes?" said Harry.
"Wait and see . . ."

"My name's Cyril," the little man went on.
"I suppose you've come to steal my chicken."

"No, I haven't," said Harry. "I'm not a thief."

"Pity," said Cyril. "You might as well pinch her;
she's not much use to me."

"Doesn't she lay golden eggs, then?" asked Harry.

"She never lays anything *but* golden eggs," said Cyril grumpily. "What am I supposed to do with hundreds of golden eggs?"

Harry could think of a lot of things.

"Why can't she lay poached eggs?" said Cyril.
"Poached eggs would be more like it . . .

. . . or scrambled eggs on toast,
with lashings of black pepper . . .

. . . or soft boiled eggs with lots
of buttery soldiers . . . "

All this talk about food was making
Harry hungry. He remembered the chocolate
bar in his pocket and was about to take a bite,
when he noiced that Cyril was getting bigger.
". . . fried eggs with crispy bacon . . ."
went on Cyril,
getting even bigger . . .

"...fat sizzling sausages, dozens of them, big as marrows. A whole pig! A small BOY!" roared Cyril, who was now enormous.

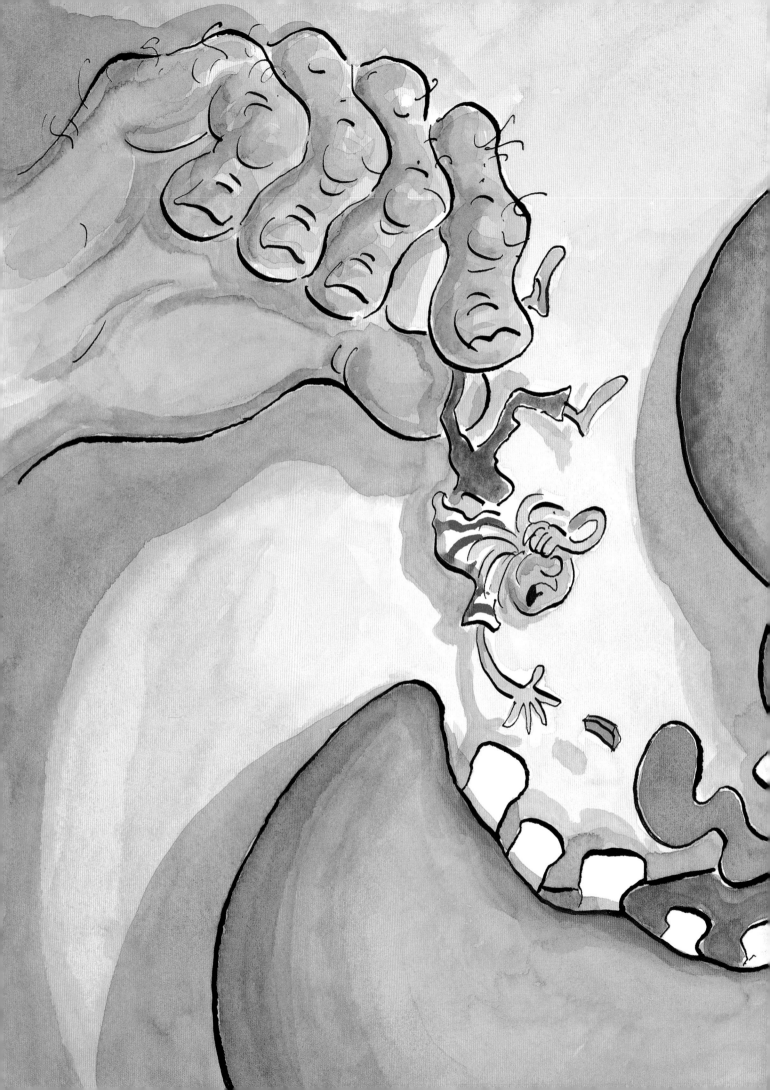

A huge hand closed round Harry and lifted
him into the air. Harry dropped the chocolate bar
and closed his eyes . . . "AAARGH!"

When Harry opened his eyes, he saw that Cyril was returning to his original size.

"Sorry about that," said Cyril. "It only happens when I think about food. The more I think about it, the hungrier I get. And the hungrier I get, the bigger I get."

"I see what you mean about being a 'sometimes' giant," said Harry. "You were enormous."

"Oh, that's not enormous," said Cyril. "You should see me when I'm *really* hungry. Sometimes I get so big, I go through the roof."

"And then what do you eat?" asked Harry.

"Beans mostly. Bean soup, bean stew, bean salad—uh-oh, I'm getting hungry again . . . Have you anything else I could eat?"

"We could go to Mum's café," said Harry.

"What's a café?" said Cyril.

"It's a place where people go to eat chips and eggs and beans and . . ." But Harry stopped himself. Cyril was getting bigger.

"Let's go," said Harry quickly,
grabbing a golden egg as he went.
He was a sensible boy.

Cyril scrambled down the beanstalk after Harry.
He was too busy keeping up with him to think about food,
so by the time they reached the café he was still a manageable size.

Harry found Cyril a seat by the window,
gave him several jam doughnuts,
and ran into the kitchen
to find his mum.

He told her the whole story in record time. But she didn't believe a word of it, not even when he showed her the golden egg.

"Harry, wherever did you get that? You take it back, right now!"

"But Mum, he'll start growing."

"Stop being silly, Harry. I'm taking these bacon sandwiches
to table four. You bring that cup of tea."

Cyril had finished his doughnuts, and the smell of cooking from the kitchen was making his mouth water. So when he saw Harry's mum with the bacon sandwiches . . .

"Help!" cried Harry's mum. "What's happening?"
"I tried to tell you," said Harry. "Quick!
Give him the bacon sandwiches! I'll get to work
on an All-day Breakfast Super Special."

While Harry cooked, his mum looked after the other customers.
By the time they came round, Cyril had eaten the bacon sandwiches
and the All-day Breakfast Super Special.

He was returning to his normal size.

"I need a nice cup of tea and a sandwich myself,"
said Harry's mum.

"I'll help," said Cyril. "I'm sorry I frightened you.
I can't help growing when I'm hungry."

Harry's mum decided she liked Cyril.

"I have an idea," she said. "We've got plenty of food here.
Why don't you come and stay with us for a while?
You can have the spare room. We've been looking for a lodger.
You could bring your chicken, too."

And that's what Cyril did.

The chicken stopped laying golden eggs when she wasn't
in the castle. She laid normal brown ones instead, which Cyril
had for his breakfast every morning.
    But Harry's mum thought it would be a shame
        to do without golden eggs altogether, so . . .

. . . one dark night, when nobody was around,
Cyril thought about yummy, scrummy chocolate bars
until he was big enough to move the beanstalk,
with the castle on top, into Harry's
back garden.

Now they could live half in the castle and half in the café.
Whenever she was back in the castle, Cyril's chicken laid golden eggs.
And although Cyril couldn't eat them for breakfast,
he had to agree that a few golden eggs help enormously . . .

. . . when it comes to affording life's little luxuries.